How Is That Working for You

MASCOT BOOKS
an imprint of Amplify Publishing Group

www.amplifypublishinggroup.com

How Is That Working for You: Overcoming Challenges When You Are Your Own Obstacle

For more information, please contact:
Mascot Books, an imprint of Amplify Publishing Group
620 Herndon Parkway, Suite 220
Herndon, VA 20170
info@amplifypublishing.com

Library of Congress Control Number: 2024906285
CPSIA Code: PRV0425A
ISBN-13: 979-8-89138-227-5
Printed in the United States

This book is dedicated to my three children, Alexis, Chanté, and David, whom I love more than words can express. You all continue to inspire and encourage me to be better and to live my best life. I hope always to make you proud and to live out Proverbs 31:28, "Her children arise up and call her blessed." Your father and I have tried to model the way, provide for you, prepare you, and encourage you all to have the courage and confidence to set your goals wisely and take action to accomplish them. My hope for you all is to stay safe, stay blessed, and live your best life. The sky's the limit! I hope that when the day arises that I am no longer among the living and have departed this life, you all can live a life where you are not your own obstacle and can teach your children, grandchildren, friends, and those around you the same.

To my parents, Cherry Ann and Clemmie Lee, thank you for providing the foundation for a strong work ethic, love of family, and adaptability. Through the many moves we experienced, you both made sacrifices each time to ensure a better life for your family. I am grateful for your support, love, patience, and encouragement. To my sisters, Jocelyn and Cheryll, thank you for always providing an ear to listen when I needed to vent, a shoulder for me to cry on, and encouraging me to keep moving forward, as I sometimes would get in my way. Beautiful Nubian queens, I love you and am thankful to you as you inspire and keep me smiling.

DEMETRIA COOPER

HOW IS THAT WORKING FOR YOU

OVERCOMING CHALLENGES WHEN YOU ARE YOUR OWN OBSTACLE

MASCOT BOOKS
an imprint of Amplify Publishing Group

OBSTACLE, FORMAL DEFINITION

[ˈäb-sti-kəl]

NOUN

obstacles (plural noun)

1. a thing that blocks one's way or prevents or hinders progress

synonyms:

barrier, hurdle, stumbling block, bar, block, impediment, hindrance, snag, catch, drawback, hitch, handicap, deterrent, complication, difficulty, problem, disadvantage, balk, curb, check, stop, interference, obstruction, barricade, blockade, cumber, trammel

—*The Merriam-Webster Dictionary*

INTRODUCTION

LIFE BRINGS CHALLENGES THAT CAN BE OBSTACLES or opportunities—sometimes both. What one chooses to do to get through those obstacles and opportunities is what shapes our lives. This may also impact the lives of others without one even realizing it. One hopes that our impact is a positive one, giving birth to opportunities and perpetual legacies. We must also acknowledge that sometimes the impact comes from *being* the obstacle. How does one recognize when the obstacle is staring back at you in the mirror? When does one then evolve and change to no longer be the obstacle?

This story begins with two women who have overcome external obstacles, maximized opportunities, and enabled others to do the same.

Deidra "DeDe" Sanderson is a forty-eight-year-old master sergeant in the United States Army National Guard. She also runs a small business as a financial consultant. She is getting ready to retire from the military after almost thirty years of honorable military service. Her story revolves around her struggle between being a workaholic and trying to figure out how to close out her long-term relationship with Uncle Sam. Many on the outside assume DeDe's love of work is the reason that she never married, but in many ways work was more of a vice or coping mechanism that she used ever since her only serious relationship experience ended at a young age.

Louise Mae "Blu" Angel is a successful psychologist with her own private practice. She started the practice after she was medically retired from the military due to severe burns and psychological wounds she sustained from an improvised explosive device (IED) in the Middle East. Blu has maintained a fairly good life-work balance living a full life serving others through her behavioral health services career, volunteering with local nonprofit organizations, and performing spoken word at local community events. Blu never got married or had kids because of her long-term feelings for her old beau, Milton, and the circumstances of distance and time.

Both DeDe and Blu have had periods in their lives when they were hindered or slowed down by their biggest obstacle: the internal force of themselves. Some of the unresolved, self-imposed obstacles that seemed to have dissipated finally rise to the surface, potentially derailing each of them from reaching the pinnacle of happiness. Compartmentalizing memories and ignoring internal obstacles seemed to have temporarily worked before, but that is no longer the case. The obstacles staring back at each of them need to finally be acknowledged and laid to rest.

PART I

DEDE

CHAPTER ONE

"GIRL, I KNOW YOU ARE COMING TO THE PARTY at Tony's this weekend." Rolanda poked DeDe with her freshly manicured false nails as she walked past DeDe's desk. Rolanda always tested the waters with her outer appearance, be it nails, hair, or uniform. DeDe sometimes wondered what Rolanda's reasons were for joining the military.

"Huh?" DeDe faked like she did not hear her coworker Rolanda, whose desk was directly across from her desk. Rolanda was a few years older than DeDe, although she looked like she was barely old enough to legally drink. Rolanda lived her life outside of her job as a human resources specialist as if she were twenty-one and would be twenty-one forever. "I hadn't thought that far ahead yet," DeDe replied.

DeDe honestly did not feel like going to hang out, as that meant she would need to find a babysitter for her son and figure out what to wear. She also knew that sharing her real reasons for not going out would only cause Rolanda to chastise DeDe about how she was young and needed to take time out to enjoy being young before it was too late. DeDe never really felt comfortable going out, mainly since she was a single parent with a young child. DeDe found enjoyment in spending time with her son and her family. She did not have to worry about fitting in and never felt awkward around her family the way she did in social situations.

"DeDe, I am going to be so mad with you if you don't come. Just this once, pretty please!" Rolanda smiled at DeDe, revealing a gold tooth near the back left side of her mouth. When Rolanda wanted something, she would beam that smile just right where that gold tooth glimmered. As if that glimmer would seal the deal for whatever it was Rolanda wanted.

DeDe exhaled and looked up from the personnel files that she was finishing data entry on. She knew that if Rolanda did not get the yes that she was looking for from DeDe, DeDe would not be able to get her work done. Completing her work tasks ahead of schedule and completing them correctly was something that DeDe always prided herself on. "All right, Rolanda, but only for a little bit. This weekend is Halloween, and I'm taking my son trick-or-treating. I still need to finish altering his pumpkin costume. Not to mention I need to work on new content for my blog."

Rolanda nodded her head and gave a satisfied wink to DeDe as she slid back behind her computer. "Thank you! I am sure you won't be disappointed." Rolanda cleared her throat and took her nail file out of the center drawer of her desk. She began manicuring her nails and cleared her throat again. "I don't know why you don't have baby daddy help out," she mumbled under her breath. "Who is this mystery man anyway?" she asked of no one in particular.

DeDe stopped and glared over at Rolanda. "Excuse me. Did you say something, Rolanda?"

Rolanda rolled her eyes and shook her head as she put her nail file down on her desk. "I said I don't know why you don't have baby daddy help you out. Your son is almost two and where is his father? You do so much for your son. You deserve more. Shoot, your son and you deserve more. It takes two to make a baby, so two should be raising said baby, not one person shouldering all the weight." Rolanda got up from her desk and walked over to where DeDe was sitting. She leaned against the desk and then put her hand on her friend's shoulder. "I'm not judging you, sweety."

DeDe grimaced, particularly since the father of her child, or "baby daddy" as Rolanda referred to him, was not a topic she discussed with anyone. When DeDe had initially discovered she was pregnant, everything unfolded rapidly and unexpectedly. Considering the circumstances, she decided it was best not to reveal the pregnancy to him or anyone else. She and Tyrell had been good friends, but DeDe had let herself catch feelings for him. She knew that he already had several children by several different women at the time, but part of her thought maybe Tyrell had just not been with the right woman. She ended up losing her virginity to him, and they did not use protection. She felt that her getting pregnant was her mistake to mend and she would make the best of it for both her and her child. Once she had found out she was having a boy, she almost talked to Tyrell about it, but she felt like there was no turning back from her decision after so many months had passed from when she had initially found out she was pregnant.

"DeDe, we don't have to talk about it, but I would not be me or your friend if I did not say what's on my mind. I understand if you are upset with me, but I love you like a sister, girl." Rolanda paused before she started to walk back to her desk. DeDe reached out and grabbed her friend's hand.

"Rolanda, I promise you one day we can talk about it, but I still need some time to process it all in my head. I appreciate you, as there are not too many people that I trust other than my family. Thank you for being patient and keeping it real with me like you do."

Rolanda tilted her head to the side. "I hear you." She laughed, squeezing DeDe's hand reassuringly. "In the meantime, I did want to talk to you about your blog. I like what you posted on the last ones. You should add in some content about investments and becoming debt-free." Rolanda began rambling. That was a good sign that the awkwardness had passed for now.

"People our age usually don't think about investing in some rims on a car," Rolanda joked. "We need your financial expertise on stocks and bonds so people can step up from cashing out savings bonds well before they mature. I don't know why they even still have savings bonds." Rolanda paused as she sat back down at her desk and glanced over at DeDe to make sure she was still listening. "I hope you are writing all these ideas I am giving you down, Boo Boo." Rolanda laughed. "Just remember me when you are rich one day! I don't need a lot, just a trip to Jamaica so I can enjoy looking at all those beautiful chocolate men over there."

DeDe laughed at her friend as she shook her head. One thing about Rolanda was that she certainly knew how to balance playing as hard as she worked. Most people missed out on the knowledge and perspective that Rolanda had because she could be a bit "extra" sometimes. They allowed Rolanda's exterior, her seemingly superficial "high-maintenance" demeanor, to deceive them.

"Now, I don't know about you, but I need to finish entering these files before the boss comes." Rolanda sighed loudly, pointing her nail file at DeDe. She opened her desk drawer and slid the nail file back into the travel manicure kit. "You know how she gets close to the weekend!" She laughed, winking at DeDe from across the room.

DeDe shook her head and chuckled at Rolanda as they both returned to completing their respective work.

CHAPTER TWO

AS ROLANDA FINISHED TIDYING UP a few things around the house in preparation for the get-together, she sighed a smile of relief. Things had been surreal for Rolanda since she met Tony at a club earlier in the year. Initially he was more interested in her than she was in him, but after going out on an initial date, Tony slowly but surely won her over with his quick wit and no-nonsense attitude. He was a few years older than her (ten years to be exact) and worked in finance and accounting.

After the two had been dating for a few months, Tony had won a trip for two to Las Vegas, all expenses and amenities paid for. While they were in Vegas, Tony proposed to Rolanda, and she accepted his proposal for marriage without hesitation. She still could not believe that they were married, and she was pretty much settled in her home with her husband. She had not really thought that she would ever find a man that she wanted to settle down with, especially so soon, let alone one who was ready to settle down with her and her quirky personality.

Tony had been married before, but Rolanda did not know much about his previous relationship since Tony made it clear that he was all about living for the future and not dredging up the past. There were questions that Rolanda had wanted to ask Tony, but she did not want to ruin the good thing that she and Tony had. They had way more good times than not-so-good. The few times that she had seen

Tony get upset, she made a promise to herself to try as hard as she could not to be on the receiving end of his anger.

"Hey, Rolanda, bring me a beer out of the fridge." Tony's deep baritone voice interrupted Rolanda's thoughts. She had not even heard him come into the house. "*Rolanda*!" Tony yelled.

"Coming, Tony," Rolanda stammered as she quickly grabbed a Stella Artois from the fridge. She took a few deep breaths during the seconds that it took to get from the kitchen toward the direction of Tony's voice.

"What took you so long, babe? You talking to your boyfriend again?" he asked accusingly. "Where is your phone? I tried calling you earlier when I was on my way home from work to see if you needed me to pick up anything." As she handed him the beer, he took it with his left hand and grabbed her wrist tightly with his right hand.

"My apologies, Tony. I was getting things ready for the get-together. I just put the food on so everything is pretty much done," she said, smiling, hoping that would calm Tony down. She pulled her phone out of her pocket, looked at it, and then looked at Tony. "I didn't get any missed calls from you, sorry. I appreciate your thoughtfulness, though."

Tony grabbed the phone out of Rolanda's hand. "Why is it locked? We talked about this. What are you hiding?" he asked, his voice getting lower in volume and his words coming out slowly as he gritted his teeth.

"Tony, please calm down. I promise I am not hiding anything. We did talk about this, and I'm still confused at why you think I'm cheating on you." She exhaled an exasperated sigh, which only made Tony angrier.

"Just get out of my face. You are pissing me off, and we are about to have company over."

As Rolanda walked out of the living room, she felt conflicted at why Tony had been acting so strangely the past few weeks. He was acting increasingly suspicious of her, and she was not sure why. She went into the kitchen to check on the food in the oven and turned the pots that were cooking on top of the stove down to low. She figured she had just enough time to go take a quick shower before she put her entertaining face on.

* * *

DeDe felt uneasy when she arrived at the party that night. From the little that Rolanda had told her about the get-together, DeDe did not expect what she saw when she arrived. *Argh*! It was a full-blown party. Cars were parked along the curb down both sides of the street and in the driveway. Rolanda and Tony had just gotten this place together a few months ago, but this was the first time they had anyone over. Tony, who was not in the military, was still a bit of a mystery to DeDe. Rolanda had not shared where or how she met Tony, yet they had suddenly taken an impromptu trip to Vegas and come back married.

DeDe generally tried not to lecture others on their decisions but had made an exception for her friend in this instance. "Rolanda, what do you know about Tony? Where is he from? What are his parents like? Does he have a job, and what is it?" These were just a few of the questions that she had asked Rolanda in an effort to get her friend to not jump into things before getting to know more about whom she was dealing with. The conversation most times would end in Rolanda waving her off and, sometimes in so many words, telling DeDe to "go get some business of your own and stop minding mine." DeDe always obliged her friend so as not to overstep. In some ways, DeDe's agreeing to come to the party was also an attempt to support her friend by getting to know Tony a little bit on her own. She felt that she owed it to her friend to give this guy a chance, especially since Rolanda had quickly promoted him from "boo thang" to husband.

DeDe found a parking spot at the end of the cul-de-sac. She stepped out of her four-door sedan and clicked the lock button. She smoothed the front of her capri shorts down and adjusted her blouse so that the sleeves covered her shoulders. The knots in her stomach got worse as she walked toward the house. She tried to remember the last time she ate. Maybe her stomach was doing internal summersaults because she was hungry.

"Wass up, shortie," a deep voice greeted her unexpectedly. DeDe turned in the direction of the voice, puzzled by whether the words were a question or a statement. Rolanda's cousin Jerome half smiled at DeDe, staring down at her from his seat on the front porch. He stood up from his seat as she walked up the porch steps. His six-foot-four frame towered over her five-foot-eleven frame. As he opened the front door for her, DeDe could not decide if he was being chivalrous or trying to take a peek at her butt.

"Hey, Jerome. How are you? Haven't seen you in a while." DeDe managed an obligatory greeting to Jerome, not waiting to hear his response.

"I'm doing good now that you are here, DeDe." Jerome grinned, licking his lips suggestively at her. "Don't have too much fun, sweety." Jerome allowed the screen door to gently shut as DeDe walked into the house, then he went back to finishing the cigarillo he was smoking.

"Hey, DeDe!" Rolanda instantly greeted her. Her voice was just barely loud enough to hear over the house music that was playing.

Several people were dancing to the music in the middle of the living room; others were bobbing their heads to the music while seated throughout the spacious area. DeDe scanned the room and saw there had to be about two dozen or more people there. DeDe suddenly felt out of place and began to regret that she had let Rolanda convince her to come out tonight. Rolanda could tell by DeDe's nonverbals that she was uncomfortable.

"DeDe, don't be like that. You just got here." Rolanda frowned. She was not letting DeDe off the hook that easily. It had taken Rolanda a long time to develop her friendship with DeDe, especially since DeDe was not in the habit of doing anything outside of work and family.

"Don't be like what, Rolanda?" DeDe asked rhetorically. She cleared her throat and backed up toward the wall that was immediately by the front door. DeDe looked like a cat contemplating an expedient exit. "You said it was just a get-together. This," she exclaimed, throwing her hands up in the air, motioning toward the groups of laughing people, "is a party. You know I don't do parties." DeDe pursed her lips in a frown, lowering her head slightly. She was agitated but did not want to cause a scene. She did not want any unnecessary attention from this room full of people she did not know.

"DeDe, I didn't know Tony was inviting all these folks. It honestly was supposed to be just a few people. Then Jerome and his crew showed up, so . . ."

Rolanda shrugged her shoulders, her eyes widening innocently. She reached over to DeDe, her words slightly slurring as she linked her arm with DeDe's. "C'mon, DeDe. Don't be a party pooper. You look so pretty tonight. Show that pretty smile." Rolanda touched DeDe's cheek. She then led DeDe over to the kitchen. DeDe feigned a small smile and straightened her shoulders a bit, trying to hide the awkwardness she had initially felt. Rolanda always had this way of making DeDe relax a bit, just enough to get a glimpse of what it was like to live in the moment.

"DeDe, I'm so glad that you came," Rolanda continued as she and DeDe walked into the kitchen. Rolanda walked over to a stack of paper plates next to several bowls and platters of barbeque, potato salad, macaroni and cheese, and other side dishes. "Lemme make you a plate, sweety." Rolanda smiled over at DeDe as she started spooning small portions of different items onto DeDe's plate. She started to pour liquor into a glass, but DeDe politely shook her head no thank you. DeDe had not drank since the night she lost her virginity to Tyrell.

After DeDe sat down at the table to eat the plate that Rolanda fixed, one of DeDe's favorite songs came on. It was a nice mellow track that started with about a minute of live bass, guitar strings, and gentle humming. DeDe closed her eyes as she listened to the familiar sounds, forgetting how a few moments ago she had started to feel angry and anxious about being duped into coming to a party. Music always seemed to calm DeDe's mind, especially when thoughts of her high school friend and first love, Tyrell, came to mind. DeDe wished that she had kept up with playing her keyboard from when she was younger. That was yet another thing that she mentally connected to Tyrell. Making music together was something they used to do before things got complicated.

Maybe she would learn to play the piano. Not like she would have the guts to play in front of people, but she would just like the comfort of knowing how to play and make music if she decided to.

DeDe finished eating her food and listened to a few more songs. It sounded like this was an album from the same group. *Nice,* DeDe thought to herself, welcoming the musical distraction. After what seemed to be the last song on the album had played, DeDe stood up to throw her empty plate in the trash. She glanced at her watch and saw that it was just after midnight. She looked around the room, wondering where Rolanda was. The party had pretty much emptied, and part of DeDe wondered where everyone had gone. Rolanda had invited her to stay until Saturday lunchtime to go over the blog. DeDe had also been considering whether breakfast the next morning would be the right time to finally talk to Rolanda about Tyrell and their son. The other part of her was ready to leave herself, but she did not want to be rude by leaving without saying goodbye to Rolanda.

DeDe headed up the stairs to where the bedrooms were. She heard what sounded like muffled crying. She gently knocked on the door. "Rolanda. Is that you? Are you OK?" She thought she heard something heavy thud, like someone had knocked an ashtray onto the carpeted floor.

DeDe leaned her ear closer to the door, listening for the muffled cry again. She heard laughter, and the music from inside the room got audibly louder. She knocked again, this time a little louder, so that if Rolanda was inside, she could hear the knock over the music.

"Rolanda, I'm getting ready to head home. I wanted to tell you good night before I head out." After a third knock and no response, DeDe paused, waiting for some sort of confirmation that someone was on the other side of the door. She debated on opening the door. Just as she began to turn the knob, she hesitated, let go, and decided against it.

DeDe turned back toward the staircase and began walking down to the living room. It had gotten pretty late, and something did not feel right. It was also well past time for DeDe to check on her son, even though her sister Lola was home babysitting. She decided that it was best for her to go home. She would call and check on Rolanda later.

* * *

On Monday morning, DeDe woke up and headed to an early morning of physical training with her unit. She had gotten her son dressed and they were in the car when she noticed after she buckled him into his car seat that he had vomited on the back of the driver seat. Nothing like toddler's projectile vomit to start out the day. Even though she had been delayed, she still made it to training early.

She arrived fifteen minutes prior to the start of the morning formalities of accountability, saluting the flag and starting a three-mile run around the military base. When she pulled into the parking lot, she looked around to see if Rolanda had arrived yet. She had not heard from her friend since the party on Friday and had meant to call her this morning before she dropped her son off at the daycare center. She hoped that Rolanda had not partied too hard over the weekend and overslept. She really did not want to try to find her friend in the darkness of the morning in the mass of people starting to get into formation. Since she still had a few minutes to spare, she decided to page Rolanda before heading to the formation area. She paged "411" to her friend with the number that they used for the day they became friends: 013196. At least the beeping and vibration from the pager would hopefully wake Rolanda up if she was not already en route.

It seemed like time stood still as DeDe waited to see a glimpse of her friend at morning formation. It crawled almost to a standstill after DeDe's own ability group had returned from running three miles and finished the cool down/stretching session. *Rolanda is usually a few minutes late just making it to formation every now and again, but that had not happened in a while,* DeDe thought.

She debated on asking their section leader if he had heard from

Rolanda, but she didn't want to get anyone worried for no good reason or rat her buddy out. There was probably a perfectly good explanation for why DeDe had not seen her friend. Maybe she went to sick call at the clinic this morning. DeDe decided that she would stop by Rolanda's place since it was on the way back to her apartment.

As she put her keys in the ignition, she put her seat belt on and adjusted her side- and rearview mirrors. She exhaled slowly and inhaled deeply for a minute, praying to God that Rolanda was OK.

When DeDe arrived at the corner of Rolanda's street, she immediately saw that the road was blocked off with police cars, ambulances, and yellow police caution tape. DeDe's stomach started to become queasy as she tried hard not to jump to conclusions about what was going on. She parked her car a few houses away and started walking toward the house. She was immediately stopped by a police officer.

"Excuse me, officer. I am a friend of the resident here. Is everyone OK?" DeDe felt an overwhelming heaviness in her throat, and her heart was starting to beat faster. Her fingers had started to feel tingly, and as hard as she was trying to control her breathing, it was proving to be a futile effort.

"Young lady, we are not at liberty to discuss information about this ongoing investigation," the officer responded. "Please go back to your car, ma'am." As he waved DeDe away from the scene, DeDe's legs felt numb, and everything around her started to sound muffled.

She tried to walk faster to get to her car before the increasingly nauseated feeling got worse. She felt like she was going into a full-fledged panic attack or impending blackout spell. She suddenly heard a voice calling out to the police officer as they walked in the direction she had just been shooed away from.

"No reporters allowed, sir," she heard the officer state.

"Officer, I am not from the news; I am from the coroner's office. Can you direct me to where the deceased bodies are? We got a call about a murder-suicide."

DeDe felt her legs go limp as she lost consciousness and fell to the ground.

CHAPTER THREE

THE SUNLIGHT FILTERED THROUGH DEDE'S CURTAINS. DeDe had not had anything to drink last night, but she felt queasy, like she had a hangover. Maybe she was intoxicated from all the crying while she was at the beach last night. In retrospect, DeDe could not recall the last time that she had a good cry like that. It felt like years, decades even, of pain and doubt had been cried out. She thought that she probably still had more in her to get out but not much more.

DeDe took her time rolling over in bed, reaching one arm out over the side onto the floor to locate where she had placed her slippers. She did not want to shock her system too much by stepping barefoot onto the cold floor. DeDe reached for the furry slippers but found them buried deeper under her bed rather than beside it. She realized she must have kicked them under there when she stumbled into bed after returning from the beach. She put the slippers on and felt a hot tear slide down her face as she looked down at them. The slippers were old and dingy, but she refused to throw them away. Rolanda had gifted them to her decades ago so that DeDe would stop wearing her basic training flip-flops as "house shoes."

DeDe smiled, remembering her old friend. She missed her friend so much. Today was even harder because it was the anniversary of Rolanda's death. No tears would ever bring her back, but it was so difficult at times to make the tears stop. Another tear slid down

DeDe's face, followed by another as she thought about how much she missed her old friend Rolanda. Rolanda had a good heart and had always looked out for DeDe.

Rolanda had been one of the few people outside of DeDe's family that DeDe had actually trusted. Sometimes she felt that she was waiting for Rolanda to come back and tell her about an event that the two of them needed to go to. DeDe probably would have been content with her nonexistent social life if not for Rolanda's persistence in getting DeDe to go out.

After Rolanda's death, DeDe had stopped going out. Instead she threw herself more and more into her military career, her consulting business, and being a mother to her son. Her social life was pretty much nonexistent. She lived to work, even sometimes to her detriment, especially lately as she got closer to closing this chapter out. The past year had been an uphill journey, almost a battle at times. She had not really been looking forward to the next chapter.

As she prepared for her military retirement, she had been working through unpacking and reflecting on the past. It seemed that her therapy sessions, especially in the past six months, had delved into a trifecta of unveiling, unloading, and unleashing. Each session felt like the weight on her shoulders was getting lighter as she symbolically let go of life's unnecessary loads that she had carried for so long.

DeDe got up from her bed and headed to the shower, not just to bring her back to reality, but more in an attempt to wash the tears and pain away. DeDe would typically give the shower a few minutes to warm up before stepping in. Today she did not pause but welcomed the cold shower as a jolt for her to move forward with her life and stop pausing to look back at the past. When she turned the water on, it blasted out from the showerhead ice cold.

The ice cold felt painful like her thoughts, particularly those about Rolanda. Thinking about Rolanda's death was painful because she always wondered if she had not left her friend's house when she did, would Rolanda still be alive? What if she had been more persistent with Rolanda about her doubts and concerns regarding Rolanda's boo-turned-husband, Tony? She wondered if Rolanda were still alive, would they be retiring together this year, or would Rolanda have already exited the military after her initial contract?

"I should talk to my therapist about Rolanda," DeDe thought out loud as the water turned warm and she finished her shower. Her next session should definitely focus on the guilt and remorse she had been holding on to all these years regarding Rolanda's death. She would talk to her therapist about her friend. It was finally time.

Rolanda was one of the few significant people from DeDe's life that DeDe had not yet spoken to her therapist about. Talking about Rolanda to someone who did not know her, who was not inside of the situation and circumstances, would allow DeDe to ease through, finally gaining closure on grieving the loss of her only friend.

As she dressed for the day, she reflected on the past several therapy sessions where she opened up about Tyrell. Surprisingly, it was not as difficult as she had anticipated. Releasing these long-held secrets about him finally made sense, shedding light on why she clung to these secrets for so long. In hindsight, it was something she wished she could redo or handle better to make things right between them, as well as for their son. She had even considered reaching out to Tyrell to see how he was doing and the possibility of revealing to him that they had a son.

DeDe pulled up to the clinic parking lot about ten minutes before her appointment. She tried to be more deliberate and consistent with her appointments, unlike when she first started therapy. Early on she had a few streaks of often canceling her in-person appointments or asking for a telephone appointment at the last minute. There were days so heavy with guilt, disappointment, anxiety, and depression that she felt she couldn't face the world, not with all the things that consumed her head and heart. Thank God that today, and the last few months, she had experienced fewer and fewer of those ugly days. Now, there were more days that she looked forward to, more days where she felt intentional about living.

As she got ready to get out of her car and head in for her appointment, she noticed a rainbow. It spanned across the sky as if it was a hologram that someone had aimed at the sky. Her eyes followed its outline from one side to the other when she noticed that a second rainbow had appeared offset from the first. She smiled up and thanked God for blessing the day with double rainbows. As her eyes came back level, she noticed something that she had not noticed before even as many times as she had been to this same parking lot. Across the street was a flower shop. DeDe made a mental note to stop by the flower shop after she finished her appointment so she could purchase flowers to take out to Rolanda's grave today.

PART II
BLU

CHAPTER FOUR

THE DAY STARTED ON A HIGH NOTE for Louisa Marie Angel. She was on cruise control for most of the day. Though she was actively involved in patient appointments, she also daydreamed in between them. She was excited more often lately as she continued to do mental spring cleaning and relationship spring cleaning. She had been doing much reflecting to get better about figuring out what her life should be, what she wanted to do, and what she needed to do.

Did something specific happen to cause this deep introspection and the refresh resulting from throwing out the garbage?

Most people called Louisa "Blu." Blue was one of her two favorite colors. The other was green. And she spelled it without the *e* because Blu Cantrell was one of her favorite singers. She did like her birth name, but people always asked questions like: Where are you from originally? That always made her laugh (on the inside, of course). The person was inherently posing the question to determine her ethnicity. She wanted to respond flippantly with, "My mama. And you?" She usually just replied, "Delaware."

Some would respond smartly to Louisa's name with, "Oh, I figured maybe you were from Louisiana or Los Angeles." Some even spelled or said her name incorrectly even after they saw it or heard it. She had been called Lois, Lewis, and even Lola. She wasn't sure how they got "Lola," but she shrugged it off.

One of the many things that she liked about joining the military was that everyone went by last name and rank. So she was Private Angel, Sergeant Angel, then Lieutenant Angel followed by Captain Angel. To think if she had stayed in the military longer, she could have been Major Angel (mic drop). She would have retired after that.

Blu had retired ten years ago after a successful career working in the military since she had graduated from high school. She did not make it to a full twenty-year retirement because she had been medically discharged after her fourth deployment to Afghanistan. During the deployment to Afghanistan, she was part of a Behavioral Health Combat Stress Team when an improvised explosive device (IED) hit the command outpost (COP). Blu ran from her deployed residence, a containerized housing unit (CHU), to the location where the team of three provided services to the two hundred deployed service members who lived on the COP. The blast resulted in a secondary explosion. Two people did not make it; the blast significantly impacted their bodies. Blu was able to pull one of her junior techs out of the aid station and away from the fire caused by the IED. Unfortunately, in the midst of all of this, Blu sustained severe third-degree burns and lung damage from smoke inhalation. She tried not to let her injuries, both physical and unseen, keep her down. She was still among the living, and some had not been so fortunate that day or during the twelve-month deployment. Blu felt that she owed it to the fallen to live her best life and allow the deployment to be a testimony.

It had been a tough transition emotionally and mentally throughout Blu's military career, both before and after this tragic deployment. Her aspirations to continue providing behavioral health services became even more focused after the deployment. On the outside, she often made it look easy. "No time for a pity party" was what she had to remind herself for the first six months after the IED blast and resulting fire.

Blu found herself reflecting more on her time in the military during her morning runs since she had retired. There was a period the first few years after the incident that she went through extensive wound care and physical therapy. During that time, being able to run was the furthest thing from her mind. Once her primary care physician officially cleared Blu to gradually resume everyday cardio activities, she eased into running with a renewed sense of purpose. She felt blessed that something she previously took for granted could be motivating and even therapeutic, physically and mentally.

Sometimes Blu hit the "off" button on her bedside alarm clock at four-thirty when it went off each morning. Other times, she woke up before the alarm clock went off, eagerly starting the day with a few miles of running and trap music blasting in her earbuds. She felt thankful to awaken to another day; some that she had cared for—including family members and others she considered part of her military family—were no longer so fortunate to say the same.

Blu tried to keep to herself. However, people tended to gravitate toward her. Some claimed it was because of her height of six feet two and her "exotic" name. She did not have many close or exclusive friends, but she was an acquaintance to whoever said hello in a kind way or responded to her hello. She was always outspoken in environments like the classroom because she loved reading and learning. She had a strong interest in English literature because of the creativity of language and expression, and she was interested in science because of the objective data and the process of hypotheses evolving into theories. Her interest in these two subjects was part of why she was excited to join the military as a behavioral health specialist. The other part was related to her interest in the human mind and human behavior. Actions fascinated her, but what inspired her was helping people understand why and how to move into their purpose.

For Blu, she felt that her purpose was to become a psychologist. She had always aspired to help others in any way that she could. Becoming a psychologist allowed her to not only help others, but also be part of a field that included so many of her interests. The combination of passion and purpose was a win-win for Blu. Joining the military allowed her to further maximize helping and serving others. The military gave her the foundation and practical experience and funded her academic journey from undergraduate degree in psychology to graduate degree in military psychology, and finally, her doctorate in clinical psychology. She had been fortunate to gain experience in traditional clinical settings as well as a wide variety of military environments during four long deployments to Iraq, Kuwait, Africa, and Afghanistan.

Knock, knock! *Knock, knock*! Blu's thoughts were interrupted by her admin assistant, Davina William, knocking on Blu's office door.

"Dr. Angel, Dr. Angel," Davina's husky voice called out. Blu rose from her chair and went over to the door, then unlocked and opened it. Davina peered at Blu over the rim of her wire-framed glasses. Blu was tall at six foot two, but Davina was a bit taller at six foot three. Patients always seemed to marvel at the height of the women upon initially meeting them. Despite their stature, once they began their initial interactions with patients, both women had their individual uncanny way of making others feel welcome.

"My apology, Ms. William." Blu grinned sheepishly. "I guess I was daydreaming for a moment. Is my 9:00 a.m. session here?"

Davina scoffed, then smiled understandingly at Dr. Angel. "Well, actually, she called to reschedule. It is still early, so I figured I would verify with you and give her a callback." Her usual formal demeanor softened somewhat as she took off her glasses and continued. "She said she wasn't feeling well enough today to make it in. She requested, if it is OK, to do a telephone appointment instead of an in-person appointment today."

Dr. Angel had already reviewed the notes from last month's session in preparation for today's session. Her 9:00 a.m. was a vet with PTSD, major depressive disorder, and anxiety. "Sure, I'm just glad she is still intentional with her therapy. Please verify with her the best phone number and let her know. Thanks." Dr. Angel smiled with appreciation at Davina.

Davina handed Dr. Angel a blue sticky note with a phone number neatly written on it. "Here you are, Dr. Angel. Here is her home phone where she requested the callback." Davina half frowned and sighed audibly. "She said that she turned her cell phone off because of all the noise." Davina paused as she got ready to head back to the front waiting room area. "I agree it is good she still wants to keep the appointment. She sounded very melancholy, like she needed someone to talk to."

"Thanks, Davina, you are the best. I am so glad that you are on my team. You always pick up on those pertinent details. I'll give her a call at this number at 9:00 a.m. then." Davina smiled and nodded her head in silent reciprocation of thanks to Dr. Angel, confirming the end of the brief conversation. Davina's black high-heeled shoes click-clacked down the corridor as she exited the hallway.

Dr. Angel turned back toward her desk to place the sticky note on her desk phone. She looked down at her watch to confirm the current time, which was 8:45 a.m. *Perfect time to run to the bathroom,* she thought to herself. She needed to stretch her legs and get her mind right before calling her patient. It was time for her daydreaming to get out of the way for the next eight hours so that Blu could do what she lived and loved to do: help others.

CHAPTER FIVE

THE DAY WAS BUSY BUT BLESSED. The clinic had been getting many referrals recently from the local VA hospital and a few within the tristate area. Most days, the atmosphere in the clinic did not feel like work was work because the team enjoyed what they were doing, the community they served, and the location. Things in Blu's life had started to align, particularly in her career, since finding an excellent office assistant in Davina Williams. Davina's credentials had already ranked well above the other candidates; during the interview, Davina's professional yet candid responses were just what Blu was looking for in an office manager as she was getting her private practice up and running.

Blu had moved to Delaware after she was medically retired. She was happy that her move back to her home state had worked out. Other times, when Blu had revisited places or people from her past, things had not always worked out. She had found that sometimes people and places had stayed the same, and the expectation was that she would change back to immerse herself into that place or person from the past. Reflecting on memories was only part of living; making new memories was the part that Blu tried to focus on more so that she didn't stumble as much on the painful memories of the past.

Blu was happy to have a win come through after periods throughout her life with one catastrophic loss after another—they usually seemed to come in pairs. Even though one of Blu's most painful memories had happened in Delaware, its familiarity and opportunities provided the ideal combination for Blu to feel like she was winning at life. The best part about moving back to Delaware was that whenever Blu wanted or needed to get away for a reprieve, it wasn't too far from her father, and there was not much snow. Well, most of the time, there wasn't much snow. Blu hated snow, but the minor amount and frequency of snow that her home state did get were acceptable considering the other pluses.

One of Blu's favorite places to visit was Texas, which had been her second choice when choosing where to plant roots for her life after the military. She was still considering moving there, but that might only be feasible in the next five to ten years. This time delay would allow her therapy practice to become more established. She also still needed to identify primary and alternate practitioners to take over.

Texas was an extended drive from Delaware, but something about the state made her feel like it was where she needed to be. She had attended college there for both her master's and doctorate as well as her military training for tech school. Any opportunities that arose to visit Texas or her friends that lived there, she took. Train, plane, automobile—Blu would make it a priority. She always felt rejuvenated after she visited Texas for some reason.

Speaking of feeling rejuvenated and revisiting people and places, Blu was so excited to see how her upcoming weekend plans to visit a particular old friend would pan out. Blu had last seen Milton Davis right before her first deployment to Iraq over twenty years ago. She worked in the hospital, but a special mission had come down, and they were looking for volunteers. Blu had volunteered for the deployment because she wanted to serve and support those serving where they needed it most. Not many in her field volunteered to deploy, let alone go to Iraq. During that particular time frame, the length of the deployments and the location in Iraq only made the list of volunteers that much shorter. Not that there were any "ideal" places or times to deploy to Iraq.

Once Blu had returned from that fifteen-month deployment, Milton (who was also in the military) had been relocated to Korea. Blu and Milton kept in touch briefly during the initial part of her deployment. That was for the first three months, but different variables on both Blu's end and Milton's slowly diminished the frequency of communication between the two from every few days to every few months. The operations tempo of the mission and outreach that the mobile behavioral health teams did to cover the area of responsibility and Milton's transition to the criminal investigation division (CID) combined with the time zone differences presented challenges that neither had anticipated.

Over the years, Blu and Milton periodically reconnected by email or social media. Their interactions became far and few between, where months would go by, then years, because of the detours each of their lives had taken. Blu always wondered if things would have been different if she had waited to volunteer for the deployment and for Milton to find out the outcome of his initial CID packet submission.

Despite the detours, distance and time had not dampened the flames of Blu's emotion for Milton. It kept them burning all these years. Milton would always have a special place in Blu's heart. Milton always made her feel seen in a way she had yet to experience with anyone else. She could not believe that she was getting to see him in person, face-to-face, after all this time.

Blu's memories of Milton were mainly of the emotions he evoked in her. She remembered his deep laugh, his voice, the feeling of safety and relaxation that she felt when she was with him. His chuckle always made her smile, but the feeling was even better because of how handsome he was in person. His smile went from his eyes, almost with a glimmer in them, to the corner of his lips. The clincher for Blu was Milton's lips; his smile reached into her and gently massaged her heart and stimulated her mind.

Recently, the two had begun to communicate more through the telephone. Social media no longer seemed appropriate for the reconnection that was taking place. They started to keep in touch more regularly, even if it was a "Good morning, beautiful" from him or a "Have a good day, handsome" from her. Their talks were getting deeper. They'd reminisce over memories of their time together, or share details about the lives they've lived since then.

It felt good, and it felt right. It did not feel like getting to know someone all over again. It felt like opening a book that one had been reading before and picking up where you left off. The only difference was that their lives were two separate books whose pages were starting to fold together; they were filling in the gaps for one another of what had transpired in each of their lives. Some gaps, Blu realized, she might not have been privy to even when they were together before she went to Iraq. Other times, she was privy to the information but had not fully paid attention to the person Milton was before. She wanted to make up for any lost time and take the opportunity to get to know Milton as much as he knew her.

When Blu was with Milton, her emotions and thoughts felt like water steadily flowing from a spigot. Blu welcomed and appreciated this feeling. The feeling of being vulnerable with another person who listened and willingly shared their trials, tribulations, tests, and testimonies.

Sometimes after they talked, Blu felt afraid that she might reveal too much and inadvertently run Milton off. She was also fearful that she would be a human IED, potentially blowing up something good.

She was not trying to jinx herself, but she had lost too many people she cared about, and it made her afraid to allow herself to go there with anyone. That same reason also made her afraid *not* to go there with Milton, even though she had always felt connected with him. She did not want this opportunity to slip past her for a second time.

Sometimes when they talked, Blu cried. It was not a sad cry, but rather a refreshing cry, cleansing all the doubt and fear away that she had successfully compartmentalized. In her profession, she believed in compartmentalizing her personal issues and emotional baggage to maintain professionalism while assisting others. Despite this, she found solace in sharing everything with Milton, confident he would not judge her. She told him that in so many words, and he echoed the same sentiments. Milton's words were like the calm after the storm that had been her life. He had gotten her through some emotionally challenging periods. She hadn't been in a relationship with a man like this in a long time—the last being with him, before she left for Iraq.

The individual nuances that Blu and Milton had were sometimes remarkably similar or overlapping. For example, she was a night owl more times in a week than not. He was a super night owl, probably because of his work in law enforcement both in the military and as a civilian.

Milton and Blu had often gone to midnight movies, which she loved. They weren't just going out to go out; they were enjoying each other and enjoying something together that encouraged more good conversations and more memories to reflect on later. The times they spent together were the foundation of even better memories, particularly when they were unexpected. If she had late-night munchies, he already knew by some weird telepathy. Even if he didn't know, he was kind enough to ask, "Hey, do you need anything? I am headed over."

Before and after Milton, Blu catered to her boyfriends' wants (or at least what she thought they wanted). In some instances, they assumed they knew what she wanted without factoring in who she was or what she actually wanted. They did not "see her," or they made her feel as if they were not interested in seeing her but rather merely interested in what she could do for them. Some did not see her because she presented another side of herself, which wasn't always an accurate portrayal of the authentic Blu.

For an extended period, Blu had doubted her worth as a woman and sometimes her value as a person. She often felt misunderstood; some people might underestimate her, or just as often, overestimate her. Sometimes she felt invisible. When she failed to find worth in herself, it caused her to try and make herself fit what she thought others wanted her to be. Or what she thought they wanted her to know or thought that she should do.

Sometimes it worked out for everyone in a good way—at least that is what Blu had convinced herself most times. Other times it did not, and Blu felt that she needed to pick up the pieces of the aftermath since it was somehow her fault that things went awry. Blu found herself apologizing to people in instances where she may not have even been the one at fault. It was often easier to go along just to get along. Most times that worked out for the other person/people involved, but it only left Blu feeling sad and genuinely blue.

Blu's favorite color was blue. Blue like the sky, but also blue like sadness. Blue like melancholy blue, or like dark sky blue behind the orange sunsets. The blue that some see but ignore. The blue the color of the ocean mixed with the green. The blue of the beach. Blu's life had shifted toward the darker shades of blue until it was almost black, a darkish blue. During those dark periods, Blu disliked light. She often took showers in the dark with the glow of a plug-in night-light illuminating just enough so that Blu could see to be safe (barely). Blu did not like seeing her reflection sometimes, and it got worse when she began to feel invisible in her relationships. Being with Milton was one of the few times that Blu did not feel embarrassed or invisible, and she did not mind the light.

Milton and Blu had even made love with the lights on before, although Blu typically did not like having the lights on. With anyone else, she preferred the lights off because she did not want them to see her flaws. The external flaws and imperfections seemed like they were snitching on the mess of a person that Blu had been. Her past was the reason why she loved helping others. She always rooted for the underdog because, more times than not, she had felt like one herself.

Blu loved helping people, but she had to learn how to help without enabling others to overly rely on her. Blu also had to learn how to help herself so that she would actually have the energy to help others at the level they needed. Sometimes Blu's passion for others was so intense that it was off-putting to some. She did not intend it to be, but that was another reason her nickname came to be an acronym—BLU: Blu loves universally. People knew Blu had a big heart, and while some embraced it, others exploited it. Milton was one who never exploited or abused her heart and often reminded her not to shortchange herself for anybody.

CHAPTER SIX

BEEP, BEEP! BEEP, BEEP! Blu's watch alarm went off, interrupting her thoughts audibly while also buzzing distinctly on her left wrist. It was 8:55 a.m. Lately, Blu relied on multiple alarms set throughout the day to keep track of her scheduled events. Blu also had to set alarms to remind her when to turn her mind off for breaks and for sleep. She had an early morning to finish packing for her trip and to close out the end of the workweek before her weekend getaway.

Blu found herself absorbing the moments, reflecting on the memories, and healing from internal and external wounds and self-inflicted and self-imposed scars. As both a practitioner and someone with personal experience—physically and emotionally—she knew that the body and mind heal and recharge through rest. Now it was time for Blu to not only compartmentalize her mental boxes but also close them up to focus on rest. She needed her energy even more these days so that she could be at the top of her game to empower others to heal.

Blu's career path toward becoming a psychologist was both rewarding and therapeutic. Blu had learned to consistently allow others, and especially herself, to replenish her lifeblood. She strived to empower others instead of enabling them. This type of mentoring and collaboration ideally resulted in individuals realizing or harnessing their worth to push through life's toils and turmoil, its joys and jams. Blu also became more discerning of the *who* and the *how*, the *when* and the *where*. The *why* was not always initially clear, but it eventually became translucent.

The clarity from considering these three *w*'s and the *how* was a strategy that helped Blu to get better about making sure that she was not pouring from an empty cup while she poured into others. You can't help others believe in themselves if you do not honestly believe in yourself. The adage of "healer heal thyself" became Blu's mantra at the beginning and the end of each day. This adage was second only to praying to God for his blessings, discernment, courage, protection, and strength.

One of the things that she prayed to God more and more lately about was strength and courage. Strength to know when to rest and let go, but also the courage to know when to move forward. With this courage and strength, Blu had to learn how to unplug, recharge, and reset by closing old chapters and not holding on to things as much as she used to. These things include grudges, receipts from over ten years ago, magazines, memories of being taken advantage of, and memories of being shortchanged or blatantly taken for granted. Those things were in the rearview; some were even on the floor of the back seat! They only served the purpose of distracting her from her present and her future.

As she looked forward to her present state and future opportunities, one way that Blu also recharged was by reflecting (but not dwelling too long) on the good memories: positive people, mentors who believed in her when she sometimes didn't believe in herself, and hobbies that gave her a sense of accomplishment and project completion yet did not feel like work. Seeing Milton again at this point in her life was an on-time bridge of the past intersecting with her present life, as well as a potential future with Milton. This was ideal timing since Blu was in a better headspace than she had been in for a long time.

Blu had fully recovered from bariatric surgery and the figurative removal of other heavy weights in her life. Blu had learned how to date herself for the last few years while also solidifying her career in her life after the military. She was more in love with herself, in a nonegotistical way, than she had ever imagined possible. She did not feel like a new Blu or a Blu with a new attitude. Blu felt like an evolved, refined Louisa Marie Angel: imperfect yet empowered and empowering others.

Blu's flight to visit Milton was departing late that night. She loved red-eye flights because they generally weren't as crowded. People were also calmer, and there was a serene, quiet environment during the flight. Blu was able to sketch in her journal or even just sleep. As the plane would touch down at the destination, Blu often stepped off her flight feeling a renewed sense of clarity and purpose. Flying was also one of the rare occasions when Blu stayed in the same spot for more than a few hours. The best part about flying was that the mission and objective were clear and straightforward. Mission: sit still, sit back, and relax. Objective: see the mission and arrive safely at the destination.

Flying was one of the few times Blu did not have her cell phone, laptop, or tablet in hand, and she did not feel worried about the time. Sometimes Blu would watch an in-flight movie or listen to classical music. She even took the time on many occasions to rub some lavender essential oil on her pulse points and allow it to work its calming and relaxing magic. Flying was one of the few places where Blu did not feel ashamed or broken. She had also gotten better about not being sad that she was by herself. How Blu felt about flying now was night and day compared to how she used to feel. It used to be that even when people surrounded Blu, she sometimes felt even more alone, like she was having an out-of-body experience.

Worse than feeling alone was wanting and needing to be alone because of all of the noise. The noise was a weird one for her. Blu loved playing loud music in the car while driving on her morning commute or during long road trips. However, if she had a traveling companion, she was always mindful that not everyone liked to hear the same thing she did. An enclosed space with another person was no place for extreme volume. On those types of drives, Blu put the radio on a neutral station: gentle, ambient instrumental jazz or gospel. Oh, and her hands were at ten and two o'clock on the steering wheel. The riding companion, the reason for the shared journey, and the destination could cause Blu to be either more anxious—and overly talkative—or less anxious—and quiet. Even without them saying anything, Blu could inadvertently absorb whatever the other person or people in the car were going through. Often Blu's tendencies as an empath absorbed the other person's energy and emotions.

The unintentional emotional absorption was one of the downfalls of Blu being an empath. Empathy was stressful for Blu even more since her fourth deployment. Her mind would create an infinite stream of mental "what-ifs." "What if something happened during the car ride, like an accident or argument? What if there was no way out?" Her mind would run through the gauntlet of what-ifs.

PART III

CONNECTIONS

CHAPTER SEVEN

"GOOD MORNING, DEDE. How have things been going?"

So much had happened just in the past week. DeDe did not know where to start, nor what she had time to share within the one-hour slot with her therapist. After the retirement ceremony, DeDe would head to Jamaica for her retirement vacation and would be gone for an undetermined amount of time. Today would therefore be DeDe's last session for a while. She debated on leading off with that in response to Dr. Angel's question but decided against it. She did not want to start the session with that kind of news of closure when it might be more appropriate to mention it toward the end of the therapy session.

DeDe inhaled deeply and then exhaled before she replied slowly, "Well, Dr. Angel, I think I am finally ready to close this chapter and start living my life outside of my work." As DeDe paused, the words seemed to hover in the air in front of her. She had thought about the finality of closing this chapter. Saying it out loud usually made her start to tear up. Today was the first time she was able to broach the subject of her upcoming transition without crying. Even so, it still felt surreal to her, but it was more tangible since the ending was so close to finally happening.

"Dr. Angel, I hope you do not take this the wrong way, but you seem to be glowing since you got back from vacation. You must have gone to Florida," DeDe joked.

Dr. Angel smiled. "Thanks, DeDe. No, I actually went to Texas. It is so beautiful there and has a different vibe than Florida."

"Oh yes, that is true. I have family that lives in the Austin area. I've been there a few times to visit my brother and his family. Texas does indeed seem to have a good vibe from what I have seen."

"That's exactly the area where I was." Dr. Angel paused, clearing her throat before she continued, "My friend just went into a partnership with a well-known restaurant owner there."

"Oh wow, too funny. My brother has been in the restaurant industry for a long time. He has a ranch there in Austin and built a farm-to-table restaurant that is pretty popular. You should check it out the next time you go."

Dr. Angel paused and cleared her throat again. "Thank you for the recommendation." There was an awkward but brief pause before Dr. Angel cleared her throat again. "DeDe, one of the things I wanted to discuss with you in today's session is that I will be transferring you over to Dr. Walsh. I will be moving out of state to expand my therapy practice."

DeDe sat up in her seat, straightening her back. "Wow." DeDe smiled, which elicited a look of confusion from Dr. Angel. "I mean, I don't want to see you go; nothing against your colleague, Dr. Walsh. The funny thing though is that I did plan on talking to you about pausing my therapy for at least a few months. I'm flying out to Jamaica after my official retirement date." DeDe paused and laughed. "You know I only purchased a one-way ticket?" Dr. Angel looked up. She was a bit taken aback by DeDe's rhetorical question. "I'm coming back, of course. I am just leaving it open on the when. Nothing planned except traveling after I retire."

"Wow," Dr. Angel replied. DeDe sat across from her therapist, looking as if somebody had lifted a massive weight off her shoulders. "Now who is glowing?" Dr. Angel asked jokingly.

Dr. Angel's tone changed back to a more serious one. "Honestly, part of me is a bit concerned about you stopping your therapy so abruptly, especially since you had not been consistent with your appointments like you were previously."

"Dr. Angel, my apologies for interrupting, but I have thought this through. I have banked money from investments for so long that it has accumulated so much interest. Between my retirement check, VA disability, and I guess all those years of 'working to the bone,' I can finally enjoy the fruits of my labor." She paused, letting out a sigh. "I do owe you an apology for missing and canceling several appointments at the last minute this past year, but it honestly got hard to even keep thinking, let alone talking about, all the things that I had on my mind and in my heart. In the past few weeks, I finally realized that I had done so much work all these years—practically all of my life—that it went well past me just being passionate about my work. I was distracting myself from feeling guilty about many different things, some of which were circumstances and situations beyond my control."

Dr. Angel leaned back in the chair and nodded her head, acknowledging DeDe's openness in a sincere attempt to encourage her to continue.

"Dr. Angel, I did not realize I had become my own worst enemy. I never realized that all these years, I have been punishing myself for things. Things that I wished I could go back and have a do-over. People that I cared about, I feel like if I had taken different actions in certain instances, they would still be here and not gone." DeDe paused, pursing her lips, fighting back tears, yet preparing for the dam to eventually burst. "If I had not left Rolanda's house that night, she might still be here. This trip to Jamaica is the trip that Rolanda and I talked about going on one day. Part of me booked my trip to Jamaica hoping that maybe when I get there, my old friend would still be alive, or even better that she was at the island already waiting for me all along."

Dr. Angel leaned toward DeDe, handing her a small box of tissues. "DeDe, it's time you forgive yourself. Forgive yourself for things that you have continued to beat yourself up about. I understand that you are acknowledging that some things are beyond your control. That is growth. You have undergone so much change in your life and throughout our therapy sessions. That growth is something to celebrate. Your action plan moving forward is part of your celebration. In your action plan, make sure that you also include forgiving yourself."

DeDe looked over at Dr. Angel through tear-filled eyes, and she began to sob. The floodgates had opened, and the tears felt like they were detoxifying a lifetime of self-deprecation, unrelenting standards, and work addiction. She went on sobbing for what seemed like forever. In a way, the tears felt timely, washing away the old regrets and pain, making way for a new life and new memories.

* * *

"DeDe, I am so glad that you took me up on going shopping. I want to make sure that I have a nice outfit for your retirement ceremony," Lola said, taking her credit card out of her purse. She inserted the card into the reader and looked over at her big sister. "What are you planning on doing with your hair? I like how you let it grow out. You have a mane ponytail again," she teased, tugging gently on her sister's brown tresses.

DeDe had her back turned to Lola as she turned the rotating eyeglass tray on the store counter. "Girl, I hadn't even really thought about that. Probably going to slick it back." DeDe ran her hands over her hair, pausing with both palms encircling the sides of her neck. She tapped her pinky fingers against her face, reflecting on the fact that soon she would no longer have to worry about how her hairstyle would fit under her military headgear. She had undergone many transitions regarding the uniform standards in the military, mainly about how service members had to groom their hair, jewelry, and females wearing makeup (to include nail polish). She would no longer have to hesitate and consider the military grooming standards and regulations when she felt like a change of pace and wanted to try a new color, a new cut, or a new hairstyle.

DeDe was itching to try something different when it came to her hair, but she was very conservative about makeup. She was not a person who regularly wore makeup, so those parts of the standards were never a big concern for her.

She was looking forward to not having to pull her hair back into a bun or cut it short. Years of perfectly groomed military hairstyles and headgear had caused her to develop traction alopecia, with the constant pressure working against both keeping her hair in place and accommodating its natural texture.

"Hello, earth to DeDe," Lola chided her big sister. DeDe had zoned out on Lola, which seemed to happen a lot more during the past year. "Are you going to get anything? I'm all done." She patted the garment bag as she draped her new purchase across her right forearm. DeDe smiled sheepishly, nodding her head. Lola linked her free arm with DeDe's, and the sisters began to walk out of the store.

"Y'all pretty ladies, have a good evening," the cashier said, clicking her chewing gum as the bell over the door jingled.

"DeDe, we need to stop by Mama's Kitchen," Lola started as

they walked toward the black sedan parked across the street from the clothing boutique. "I skipped lunch, and my stomach is growling like a grizzly bear."

"OK," DeDe replied. She clicked the button on the car's remote start.

"DeDe, are you sure you're OK? You have been kind of quiet and spacey lately. What's up, sis?" Lola asked as she buckled her seat belt. She placed her hand on DeDe's shoulder.

"I'm good, Lola. Just tired, probably because of daylight savings time. The time change always throws my sleep off." DeDe glanced in the rearview mirror, catching a glimpse of her reflection. Fortunately, Lola could not see her eyes as DeDe tried to fight back the tears. She didn't want her baby sister worrying about her, especially since there wasn't anything wrong. DeDe had been reflecting a lot because things seemed to finally be shifting toward being right. She was retiring and headed to Jamaica soon for her retirement vacation. It would be hard to explain to her sister that she wasn't crying because she was sad, but because she finally had closure and a new beginning.

Lola started to say something when her cell phone rang. DeDe reached over and turned the radio volume up, slightly thankful that one of her favorite songs was on repeat. She needed a distractor to keep the floodgates of tears from starting. She began to hum and bob her head to the music as she pressed down on the car brake, shifted the car into drive, and transitioned her foot over to the accelerator.

"Hey. Yeah. Um-hum. Of course. OK." As quickly as the call had come through, Lola had said a few words and ended the call. "Oh, don't forget we are going to Mama's Kitchen. And you know this is my jam right here, so we have to turn this up." Lola turned the volume knob up just enough that the windows vibrated slightly from the bass.

She began to dance along with the music as DeDe sang the words.

"DeDe, can I do something quick with this bird's nest you have going on?" Lola asked as DeDe pulled into the parking spot behind the family's restaurant.

"Lola, stop being silly. I was going to stay out here while you go in. I'm too tired and don't feel like staying up in there all night." DeDe placed the car in park, leaned back in the driver's seat, and tilted her head back on the headrest with her eyes closed.

"Oh no, you are not sitting out here in the car! Come on, ole lady. Stop being antisocial. You can come in and say hello. Mama would beat you and me if she heard you were here and didn't come inside," Lola shrieked, then quickly began to whisper. "Come here; let me fix your hair really quick."

"Girl, get off me!" DeDe swatted Lola's hands away. "Fifteen minutes. You said you just wanted something to eat." DeDe unbuckled her seat belt and sighed, exasperated at the persistence of her sister. She knew that Lola was partially correct, although a bit overly dramatic. Lola would probably be even more dramatic and persistent if she knew that her sister had not seen their mom for the past few weeks. Between the busy hours at the restaurant and DeDe putting in extra time over the past few weeks to close things out with her replacement, the weekly brunch she and her mom usually shared had shifted to once every couple of months over the past year. The two women barely got a chance to speak for more than a few minutes on the phone because of their opposing schedules. DeDe made a mental note that she would get back on track with spending more time with her family once she retired, especially with her mom.

DeDe did not even recall getting out of the car let alone walking to the door of the restaurant. Her thoughts were interrupted with,

"*Surprise!*" The sudden rush of party noisemakers and a sea of smiling faces caused DeDe to pause in her tracks. She straightened her back and could not help but smile. Lola had set her up well! DeDe had zoned out again and had not even noticed that Lola had loosened DeDe's messy bun, releasing curls onto DeDe's shoulders.

"C'mon in here, baby!" her mom bellowed as she led her daughters into the restaurant's central area. DeDe's family had transformed it into an oasis with fake palm trees, a beach backdrop, and island music.

"Is that curry chicken I smell?" DeDe asked, sniffing the air and smiling at the same time.

"It sure is," replied a deep voice from behind DeDe. She already knew whose voice it was before she turned around.

"Theo! When did you get here? I thought you weren't going to be able to make it." DeDe hugged her big brother, who stood six feet seven. It had been several years since she had gotten to see him since he lived in Texas with his growing family and was busy running a popular farm-to-table restaurant. As DeDe hugged her big brother, she felt a sense of comfort come over her. What a surprise this was, awesome and unexpected.

"Do I get one of those as well?"

DeDe released her hug just enough to turn to see where and who was posing the question.

"T-T-Tyrell?" DeDe blustered. DeDe's mind was a complicated ball of confusion, and there was a sharp pain in her chest.

"Surprise!" Lola exclaimed, grinning from ear to ear until she saw the color draining from DeDe's face. Her grin turned to a look of confusion as DeDe turned and walked out of the room. "What did I miss?" She turned to Tyrell, hoping he could shed some light on her sister's reaction to seeing him.

CHAPTER EIGHT

"DAVINA, THANK YOU SO MUCH for coming all the way out here to pick me up. I could have taken an Uber!" Blu exclaimed as she walked over to hug Davina, who was walking from the driver's side to open the liftgate for Blu to throw her luggage into the back.

"Sis, you know I was not about to let you ride back from the airport today with all these Sunday drivers on the road! Plus, I want to hear all about your trip, *and* I have something I want to talk to you about. I figured once you got back to the office tomorrow, things would be back on and popping. You would probably only have time for our patients."

Blu slowly closed the liftgate as she grinned at Davina, particularly because of her statement about "our patients."

"Girl, let's get in this car before the meter maids come to try to shoo us out of this area," Davina said, mirroring Blu's smile with her own. They both laughed, nodded in agreement, and hurried into the car.

Blu eased into the front passenger seat, put on her seat belt, stretched her legs out, and kicked her heels off her feet. One of the great things about Davina being tall like Blu was that her car had ample legroom that made for a very comfortable ride. As she relaxed, she grinned, pleased that Davina even had the heated seat already warmed up to the optimal temperature.

"Davina! I wish you had gotten to come on the trip. I cannot wait for you to meet Milton! He is coming here next month, so hopefully, we can all get together for dinner while he is visiting."

Davina eased her tall frame into the driver's seat, buckled her seat belt, and eased back into the traffic lane, headed out of the airport toward the expressway. "Um-hum, that would be nice," Davina stammered, clearing her throat. "I have to check my calendar," she responded distractedly.

"Oh," Blu replied, a bit taken aback that Davina did not seem excited about the opportunity to finally get to meet Milton.

"How was your flight?" Davina asked, quickly changing the subject.

"The flight was good, uneventful. I slept through it. It seemed so quick," Blu replied. "Shoot, from thinking about riding Milton's motorcycle while I was in Texas, I woke up thinking I was getting off the bike and not the plane!" She laughed and sighed, leaning back more in her seat, closing her eyes. Something about thinking of being on the back of Milton's bike, riding on the highway, made her feel like she was mentally back there.

"That man does something to me, Davina! Riding on his bike made me feel so connected to him, as if I could sit there forever with my chest on his back and my arms wrapped around his waist." Blu opened one eye to look over at Davina to gauge if her friend was even listening to her ramblings about the love of her life. She seemed so distracted, Blu wondered if something was wrong. Did she somehow know about the news that Blu was going to share at the Monday morning team meeting? Blu closed her hazel eyes and turned her head up toward the ceiling, leaning back in her warm seat. She smiled and let out a sigh, deciding to just enjoy the moment.

There was an awkward silence for most of the ride before Blu ended up falling asleep. The drive from the airport was about forty-five minutes, so Davina figured that Blu would probably fall asleep. As Davina turned off the expressway, she was glad there were plenty of stoplights for the rest of the ride to Blu's house. Hopefully that would prolong the car ride long enough for Davina to gather up the courage to talk to Blu about something she had wanted to discuss for quite some time now.

Blu yawned and opened her eyes. She smiled at Davina, grateful for the short but much-needed nap. Blu refocused her eyes and sat up in her chair. She cleared her throat and began to speak. Just as Blu began to speak, Davina also began to speak. "I have something to tell you," they both simultaneously blurted out. Both women laughed, surprised at the timing.

"You go first," Davina said, smiling. She almost felt that she was off the hook, especially since she still was not quite sure if it was the right thing or appropriate time to tell her. She had already procrastinated on talking with Blu about this thing for the past few months, so a few more minutes (or hours) wouldn't hurt. Maybe she would regain her confidence after Blu got out all she wanted to discuss.

Davina liked hearing Blu talk, especially when she was driving. Something about Blu's voice was so very comforting. She was always amazed at how Blu articulated her words. She was even more surprised when Blu had shared her experiences of being referred to speech therapy several times as a child and as an adult.

"Aww, you go first, Davina! I forgot you said when I was putting my bags in the back that you had something to talk about. I am so sorry." Blu touched Davina's arm apologetically. Davina shifted her arm nervously from where she had rested it on the center console.

Fortunately for her, Blu did not seem to notice. "What is it? New man or an *old* man that you are finally telling me about?" Blu chided.

Davina swallowed and strategically turned her head toward her side mirror to check traffic on the road. "Girl, puh-leeze!" Davina laughed uncomfortably. "You go ahead, I probably need to concentrate on getting us through this Sunday afternoon traffic. It will be easier to do if I am not the one talking." Davina clicked downward on her turn signal, signaling to the other drivers that she was transitioning over to the far-left lane. She steered her Lexus over and eased onto the gas.

"OK, OK. Well, I received an email Friday about extending the practice to Texas. Apparently, with the increased referrals from the Veterans Affairs hospital, the community-care providers there in Texas are struggling to keep up with the influx of patients. One of my colleagues that I met at a TBI conference last year had been looking to expand his practice back on the East Coast so he could be closer to his mother, who is ill. He figured it would be too much to run the practice in Texas and on the East Coast, especially with the increased referrals, so he reached out to me to see if I might know anyone who might be interested."

"Wow, he doesn't know anyone that is in Texas in his network to hand over the reins to?" Davina queried. She looked over briefly at Blu and could honestly say that she had not seen Blu this excited about anything in a long time. "It sounds like you would be doing what he admits that he couldn't do: running two practices in two different locales."

Blu smiled and nodded her head. "I thought about that, as well as about you and all that you have done with keeping our office flowing. The two part-time providers that I brought on board last year seem to be getting into the groove of things, and we could bring on an assistant for you to be the office manager. What do you think?" Blu paused and looked over at Davina, trying to see if any nonverbals could hint at how Davina felt about the idea.

"Blu," Davina started and then cleared her throat. "Dr. Angel, I would have to give it some thought. It is a lot to take in so unexpectedly." Davina half frowned in deep thought. She looked into her rearview mirror while simultaneously viewing Blu's reaction from out of her peripheral. Part of Davina was taken aback by the news and the prospect of Blu being in Texas more, especially the thought of not having the chance to work alongside her regularly. Blu was the main reason why Davina had applied for the position and had continued to work there. They made a great team, and Davina honestly was not ready to have Blu hundreds of miles away.

Blu looked at Davina, puzzled and somewhat taken aback that Davina was not as excited about the news as she was. Blu felt as if she had missed something, and now it felt awkward to pose that question out loud in the confined space during the remaining drive. Maybe Blu was overthinking it. "OK, Davina. I understand. It is a lot to process at one time. I respect that." She paused to allow Davina time to respond. Davina looked over at Blu, revealing a quick but sincere smile of thanks.

Blu turned in her seat, placing her hand slightly on the center console. "So, you still haven't told me what you wanted to talk to me about." Blu smiled, hoping that this modest attempt to transition the conversation would potentially ease the awkwardness in the air.

"Umm, it's OK. I need to stop at the gas station up ahead. I drank too much sweet tea earlier," Davina replied.

* * *

Davina had debated on how to say goodbye to Blu. She had tried several times over the past few weeks to push past her feelings, but she felt like she was prolonging the inevitable. She had spent time carefully crafting her formal letter of resignation. She had read and reread it several times before she placed it into the manila envelope. She had a second, sealed dark blue envelope with a handwritten letter inside. She had handwritten "Blu Angel" with a black calligraphy pen on the front of the smaller envelope. She had not sealed the manila envelope yet because she needed to use her office keys one last time before placing them inside the larger envelope.

Dear Louisa "Blu" Marie Angel,

Getting to know you during the time that we worked together was an experience I would never have imagined and will never forget. You are one of the kindest people I have ever met, selfless to the point of almost not having enough left for you, but somehow you do. You use your passion for authenticity and sincerity to do the right thing for the right reasons instead of just to make yourself look good—this is an art that many hope to master. I knew this about you when we were back in high school. I wish I had more courage at that time to approach you and get to know you, as that would have given me more time to learn about the beautiful Blu that I always saw.

Thank you for the opportunity to work with you, learn from you, and fall in love with you. Plenty of times in the past year, I almost told you how I felt about you, but the more you shared about Milton, the more I knew that he was the other piece of your heart and always would be. I could not in good conscience come between that or do anything that would jeopardize our friendship. To have known you has been a treasure, and I would have never expected to find an even more precious treasure of loving someone with such a beautiful heart and spirit as you possess.

I wish you the best of luck in your next chapter and am so glad that you are finally stepping out to receive the full version of love you deserve. Allow yourself to continue to be vulnerable with him, to love him fully, and to allow him to love you fully. You have spent so much of your life helping others find their happiness, and now you have genuinely found yours. Enjoy, my friend.

Sincerely yours, Davina

* * *

Three months later, Blu was happy to have finally gotten rid of all the moving boxes. Everything was finally unpacked and in a place that would probably be its home for a while. It had taken Blu a bit longer to get settled in than she expected, and it had not been as smooth as she thought it would be since she had been sick the past few weeks. Milton finally convinced her that she needed to go to the doctor to make sure that it wasn't something more than just her allergies. Her friend, Teresa, had joked that Blu wasn't allowed to get sick, since Teresa was sick enough for the two of them.

"Good morning, beautiful." Milton leaned down, kissing Blu in the crook of her neck. "I woke up, and you were already out of bed. What are you doing up so early, woman?"

"Honey, I was trying to get these out of the way and down to the curb for the recycling truck before you got up," Blu answered as Milton's eyes caught sight of the row of moving boxes forming in one corner of the living room. She attempted to rise from the couch but quickly caught herself from falling. For a few seconds, she saw stars in front of her eyes and felt nauseous.

Milton strode quickly toward Blu, catching her arm and leading her back to a seated position on the couch. "Woman, I told you about doing too much. You are going to hurt yourself. I'm here. You don't have to do all this by yourself. I can't have you passing out from exhaustion. You have barely been here six months yet."

Blu looked over at Milton, embarrassed but grateful that she was here with him. He reached over and stroked her cheek with his hand.

"I'm going to see the doctor today. I procrastinated too long on setting up my new primary care manager since I moved here, but better late than never," Blu stated.

Milton stood up from the couch and walked toward the kitchen island to get Blu a glass of water. "When did you have time to make breakfast? I was going to make you breakfast," he stated as he bit into a turkey sausage link. He smiled and shook his head, heading for the fridge for the orange juice and water pitcher. "I'm going to have to spank that soft butt later, hardhead," he teased. He didn't notice that Blu had slowly gotten up from the couch and walked behind him. She circled her arms around his stomach and leaned her head into the center of his back, turning her head to the side.

"I love you, Milton," she said, smiling. "I hope you can forgive me for not telling you and showing you that all those years ago."

Milton placed the orange juice carton back into the fridge and the water pitcher on the countertop. He then turned around, facing Blu. She stood just a few inches shorter than his six foot four frame. At that moment, her words made her seem taller. "Everything happens for a reason and a season. Nothing to forgive. I loved you then, and I love you even more now."

Buzz, buzz. Blu's watch vibrated, interrupting the sweetness of the moment. Milton tilted Blu's chin up as he leaned down to kiss her.

Blu ignored the buzzing on her watch as Milton's lips trapped Blu's bottom lip. She kissed him back. Blu felt at peace as if time and space had paused. They stood in the middle of the kitchen, enjoying the feeling of each other in the same space—no obstacles, no challenges. No longer transient and geographically separated, but finally together.

CHAPTER NINE

"LADIES AND GENTLEMEN, the ceremony will begin in five minutes. Please silence your electronic devices and take your seats. Thank you."

How many times had DeDe been the one to speak these words? How many times had DeDe heard that during numerous military ceremonies—the retirements, awards presentations, promotions, and change of command ceremonies? Today was different because DeDe was not the mistress of ceremonies, and she was not seated in the audience reaching for her cell phone to double-check that she had placed it on silent (or better yet, had turned it completely off). DeDe was seated on the stage in the third row among two dozen other retirees.

Today's retirement ceremony would be DeDe's last ceremony in her military service uniform. She smiled as she smoothed the front of her skirt and placed her hands firmly on top of her thighs. She could not believe that she had made it to this day.

As the ceremony began, DeDe's thoughts drifted briefly. She almost felt as if she was watching herself from the audience. She was poised and waiting for each of the respective cues just like they had rehearsed several times. A subtle smile played at the corners of her lips as she effortlessly maintained her composure throughout the ceremony. The former DeDe was always nervous at events like this, overthinking the what-ifs of Murphy's Law interfering with something that was to be respectful and executed with precision. Each of the key actors in the ceremony—those who were visible and those working behind the scenes—had their respective parts to ensure that each ceremony flowed accordingly. The precision with these types of ceremonies was never by accident, but rather the outcome of careful planning, rehearsals, and scripts.

DeDe waited for the rehearsed cues of each retiree and their family member standing up sharply from their seat and executing precise facing movements. DeDe had prepared herself mentally for this day; part of her felt sad during the rehearsals as she was the only retiree in this group who did not have a significant other standing by her side.

On the day of the actual event, DeDe forgot about her sadness for those brief moments of the actual ceremony. She looked out into the audience where her son, siblings, parents, Blu, and Milton were seated. They all were sitting together five rows from the stage. Her mom blew her a kiss, while her son gave her a thumbs-up; he was grinning from ear to ear.

Today was closing the chapter on DeDe's military career, saying farewell to her long-term relationship with the military. The military had been the love of her life for so long. Now it was time for her to close out a long yet fulfilling career that had spanned more than half of her lifetime. It was now time for DeDe to begin a new chapter of living that no longer centered on the military or work.

* * *

As DeDe gazed out into the horizon, she entertained the idea of walking toward the water until she could walk no more. However, her legs felt like cement, her mind felt noisy, and her eyes felt dry from crying. She took her sunglasses off of her puffy, tear-stained face and stared straight into the sunset. The glow of orange and yellow seemed to move upward in the sky. It was as if the clouds beneath the sun were lifting it while simultaneously encouraging her to stand up from where she was seated in the sand. She was almost hesitant to stand because she was afraid that she might fall.

She inhaled as she mustered enough strength to attempt to lift her tired body upward. The sensation in her lower extremities was starting to return. Her knees were still wet from the tears she had cried while hugging them close to her chest. She laid her legs flat on the ground and crossed her left leg over her right ankle. She then dug her right heel and elbow into the ground to leverage herself up. Her foot slid across the sand, but she quickly regained her footing. Although her legs were wobbly, she continued to rise slowly but surely. She had been sitting on the beach so long that she had lost track of time . . . or maybe she had not lost track of time but rather wished she could go back in time.

There were so many things that she wished she could do over or do better. Then again, if one situation or circumstance had a different outcome, it may have a domino effect on other things. Part of her wanted to be done with it all. Then she would not have to think about the knowns of the past and the unknowns of the future. She had been to this place before. Not in the physical sense but rather emotionally at a critical point. A point when she was not sure if she could continue moving forward, or even if she wanted to.

She had contemplated numerous times the permanent decision of life's finality based upon temporary circumstances. Fortunately, she never followed through when her mind went to that dark place. Most of the other times were because somehow, at an opportune moment, she would hear a sound that jolted her back into the reality of pushing through whatever the obstacle was. Sometimes the sound was random, like the telephone ringing from a wrong number or her watch buzzing with a stick figure reminding her that it was time to stand.

Today her reminder was internal. It needed to be. She began humming as she looked at the sun and started walking toward it. Words began to take the place of the humming. She began to repeat them silently to herself, then out loud:

One day I will realize that I *am* blessed.

One day I will see that I have passed *his* test.

When he says, "Well done, thy good and faithful servant."

One day I will. One day I will.

One day I will cease to rely on what I do.

One day I will cease to rely on what I want to be.

That day is today because I finally realize that the obstacle all along was me.

ACKNOWLEDGMENTS

I GIVE HONOR TO MY HEAVENLY FATHER first and foremost for life, lessons, and blessings. I have been blessed by God, who has sent me angels to help keep me from going down the wrong path. If (and when) I did digress down the wrong road, God sent mentors to help guide me back on track and battle buddies to walk through the journey of life together so that we did not have to do it alone. So many others have allowed me to continue to move forward and do better as a soldier, leader, mother, friend, and person.

To my number one superhero, my earthly father, Clemmie Cooper, who during his lifetime always pushed me toward being my best and often tried to mentor me toward not being my own obstacle. My only wish is that you were still alive to see that I finally finished what I needed to finish so that I could finally let go and begin to live.

I also want to acknowledge my mother, my children, sisters, friends, and mentors who inspired me to finally give birth to this book. I had considered different versions of the book's topic of obstacles and had particularly struggled the past six years to gain the courage to continue moving forward with my dream of becoming a published author.

Thank you to my children, who provided feedback on different parts of my book, inspiring me to break through my writer's block. You allowed me to feel comfortable sharing my words and feelings with you as I worked through this project. Your candor and input always amazed me during those moments as each of you individually shared your thoughts and suggestions. I am so proud of the insightful and candid young adults that each of you are growing into.

Thank you to my siblings for all the memories. You all have been the continuity that reminds me where we came from, and that we had more good times than not. Thank you for being there in each of your respective ways, even when I sometimes would get in the way. I love you and am thankful for your inspiration and the blessings your individual lives have revealed.

To my nieces and my nephew, I am so proud of you and grateful for the memories and inspiration you all provide. Even with the geographical distance that has always been there because of my military and other job-related moves, it feels like you all are always nearby. Continue to be and do better each day and live your best and safest lives. I am so proud of you all as your futures shine so brightly.

To my extended family of cousins, aunts, uncles, your offspring, and our family members who are no longer living, I am thankful for the inspiration that each of your lives provides, not just to me but to those around you whose lives you have positively impacted. I am forever grateful and thank you all for your encouragement, holiday cards, and updates.

To my military family that is so geographically widespread, time and life have continued to make me appreciate more and more joining the military in 1998 and staying the course through 2018. Although several years have passed since I retired, the lessons of comradery, mentorship, life, selfless service, and personal courage continue to be revisited, reflected upon, and paid forward. I have been blessed with several great mentors who have provided life and leadership lessons.

Thank you! Many of you believed in me when I did not and held my feet to the fire when I was not living up to my potential.

For those that I may not have mentioned by name, please know that I am thankful in more ways than I have words or pages to express. I love you all, and may you continue to be blessed and to be a blessing.

ABOUT THE AUTHOR

DEMETRIA LATRICE COOPER was born in Mississippi. She primarily grew up in Brooklyn, New York, but also lived in Oklahoma, Chicago, Illinois, Louisiana, Wilmington, Delaware, and Pennsylvania. Demetria graduated from Fort Hamilton High School in Brooklyn in 1996 and is the second oldest sibling with an older half-brother and two younger sisters. Demetria is the proud mother of two daughters, ages twenty-four and twenty-one, and a seventeen-year-old son.

Demetria's professional background includes service to the nation with twenty years of honorable military service as a medic/ EMT-B and a senior army leader. She served at nine duty stations, including Hawaii, New York, Fort Myer, Virginia (The Old Guard), Fort Jackson, South Carolina, Fort Riley, Kansas, Fort Bragg, North Carolina, Fort Eustis, Virginia, and Louisiana. She returned to Fort Jackson as her last duty station before she retired from the military in 2018. During her military service, she also completed two overseas military deployments. Her first was a fifteen-month deployment to Sadr City in Baghdad, Iraq (2008–2009), as a senior medic within a military police company, and the second was a ten-month deployment to Camp Buehring, Kuwait (2015–2016), as the satellite site manager for clinical military operations. After retiring from the army, Demetria has served as a nonprofit regional program manager in both South Carolina and Hawaii and has been deployed overseas as a civilian to

Kuwait and Iraq. She has also worked for the federal government as a civilian employee and a subcontractor. Demetria currently works for the government in the role of Training Specialist (Facilitator) for the United States Army Master Resilience School.

Demetria is a lifelong learner with educational accomplishments that include a master's degree in public administration and a graduate certificate in health services management. She also holds various professional certifications as a Certified Associate Project Management (CAPM), Certified Career Coach, and Certified Life Coach with specialties in Confidence Coaching, Forgiveness Coaching, Spiritual Coaching, and Therapeutic Art Coaching. Demetria enjoys traveling, reading, writing, listening to music, and spending time with family (and a small core of key friends/extended family). She continues to work toward not being her own obstacle as she aspires to consistently live her best life through proper life-work balance.